$2X^2$

Martine Bellen

BlazeVOX [books]

Buffalo, New York

Book design by Geoffrey Gatza
Back cover painting of author: *Wonder Wheel (MB)* by James Graham

First Edition
ISBN: 9781935402213
Library of Congress Control Number 2009944209

BlazeVOX [books]
303 Bedford Ave.
Buffalo, NY 14216

Editor@blazevox.org

publisher of weird little books

BlazeVOX [books]

blazevox.org

2   4   6   8   0   9   7   5   3   1

B   X

For the lifeguards of Ditch Plains

& for James

Table of Contents

$$2X^2$$

Chapter 1

Lots of senseless sleights of hand that add up to nothing but wasted time. That's how I'd describe the card game I invented as a child. The real kicker was when I'd sense my opponent was out of steam, and I'd turn her attention to a face-down card that I had given her hours before, when the game first began, and which I called "bank." I'd wrap up the game by telling her to look at her bank—highest number wins.

"And what about all I've accomplished over the last hour, two, five, seventy years?"

"Highest number wins. That simple, no arguing."

I was ten when I created my game. I had been lonely ever since. Today I stopped feeling lonely. Today I found my twin: Rona Z.

My thinking can be described as mathematical, wordless, often complemented by mental images that offer solutions to problems.

Today as I was reading the *Times*, I came across an article about her. "Ms. Rona Z concludes that before 1990, only one-fifth of American spies described ideology as the reason that they committed treason." Four-fifths did it for bucks, for the American dream. Present trends suggest spy incentives have shifted and cash no longer turns an agent double.

Doppelganger or *double goer*. Double doer. Do gooder. A ghost following the living. A counterpart. Counterpoint.

The article continued, "Since 2000, none of the eleven identified spies have received payment for their espionage."

Even before my card game, I'd been obsessed with twin theory.

First Mother was on fertility drugs when I was conceived, so biologically I'm predestined to have high twin expectations, though, sadly, I landed on a foreign shore after the womb. On another island. My other is Rona (I'm Nora). And in typical twin fashion, it's my lot in life to look for her.

Look at her

    At me through her / her through me

Cast as two halves of one.

Have you noticed that more twins than ever are being born?

The father of Monster Slayer and Child of Water spent much of his time carrying the sun across the sky. The twins—left alone a lot, what with their dad always slinging around the sun—went searching for him. Twins are always searching. Once Father was found, he insisted he'd never been lost. "Wah! Wah!" the two whined. To shut them up, Father equipped them with monster-fighting gear so that they could slay monsters throughout the universe and within themselves. They went off on separate paths, but no matter how distant they appeared to be, they always found themselves just a shout away from one another.

When I created my game, I managed to lose any and all friends throughout the universe (and within myself). I became so lonely I doubted my twinship. Until I read about Rona.

Not to brag, but Rona Z is a trusted counselor to the Director of State Security, so she's a diligent student of the practices of spyhood. She heads up the Secrecy in Government project and, in order to stay current on spycraft, she's a member of the Confederacy of International Nonlinear Scientists. She recently gave a particularly well-received paper about cloud fractals obscuring the peak of Mount Fuji at the International Nonlinear Science Conference in Tokyo.

Random theory. Synchronicity. Karma. Shadow myths.

Shadows occupy land at the periphery of vision and disintegrate, or move between walls. Walls are constructed by landowners to keep away intruders. So my card game was a wall. My beliefs, all walls.

If a wall falls…if a bomb explodes…piggy huffs and puffs

> A siren or call of distress. Cicadas.

Nora saw a shadow and whispered, "Stay there." It lingered for several seconds before disappearing. She had an accompanying feeling of dread. (Sometimes I call myself "Nora" rather than "I" or "me." Just so you know, it's still me. It's all me.)

Nora (see what I mean? still me) studied the paper written by Rona for the International Nonlinear Science Conference in Tokyo. It investigates electromagnetic fields, which sometimes interfere with the functions of the temporal lobe/time lobe. Love. And then what happens?

> Birds fly through water. Feelings of being
>
> > Lost.

Was Rona inferring that one is born into a collective group and spends one's life regathering what one already knows, *who* one knows, in search of one's intuitive nonsensical senses?

For instance, when you think of someone, often the person phones you. Of course he does, bearing in mind that the Watchers—the Corporation and Signatories—spy on us regularly. Maybe they're our dead ancestors, or shadows, or dreams, or our collective conscience, or even our consciousness (our governing board that directs policies). No idea, but I know they're here. Don't you?

Or maybe they're foreign agents. Spies.

How do we find the members of the Board of Trustees? We secrete pheromones, chemical substances that elicit a specific behavioral or physiological response in another animal of the same species. Not aware of it ourselves, we smell out our family, similarly to the way felines use scent-marks to recognize theirs. The units of our extended Corporation have scent-marks imprinted on them so that we can recognize one another.

At the top of a cat's mouth is a mechanism that the community of scientists doesn't understand, but which permits cats to analyze air molecules that are inhaled through the mouth rather than the nose. There are several hypotheses about why cats have this "Jacobson's organ." One is that they use it to smell pheromones. We start by ever so slightly opening our mouths and keeping them open.

(Our eyes

(Our hearts

(Our minds

Ever so slightly

A problem with living on this island is that the ferry seldom runs and one can become too introspective, reducing thought to bare mathematical bones. So, for instance, if you're a character in a novel, searching for your double or your collective selves and the ferry comes rarely—and when it does arrive, there's no warning—how do you act like a character in a rational novel that's built on conflict, with a narrative arc and denouement, and move out of your deep interior universe in which you are all characters, the author, and the poet? A spiritual awakening is like opening your Jacobson's organ to find yourself in a fresh book that you know nothing about. That's what's happening to me.

Chapter 2

Once she appeared in the paper, it was no surprise that Rona came to my island/my mind. The earth has an eerie intelligence.

Setting out on a quest to learn one's identity is a popular theme for twins. Twins from the Acoma Indian tribe face many dangerous trials in pursuit of the answer to "Where do I come from?" or to the more essential question, "Who am I?" Each twin dies, only to be brought back to life by his brother. In the end, they learn that they had different fathers, one immortal and one mortal. Because the twins did not know which of them had the immortal father, they protected one another forever.

Part of each person is immortal and part mortal. Part of each lives forever and part dies.

I believed that Rona recognized me at the café. Our almond eyes. Her flesh a soft yellow, like mine. We're the same height, same weight—average;

we could be anyone. And of course, I'm left-handed and she's the right-handed twin. Though we share a biological mother (First Mother), we have different second mothers, as well as different fathers. Mine clearly is the mortal one: hers, a sneaky immortal like Zeus. Hence her call to pursue a life of spying.

The café on the island is the meeting place for last-call acquaintances and first dates, where drug dealers slide stealthily across the wide-wood-panel floors, searching for takers and givers, those whose obsessions dominate their dreams. The café's patrons move tentatively between the mahogany tables and brokers of the night (as the sun rises, night- and daytimers overlap). Ambient music gets swallowed up by seductive whispers and throats clearing awkward phlegm and hissing Italian espresso makers. People on the island dress for the café. Not all-out get-up-and-go gear, but one patron might flaunt his most private tattoo, another her great grandmother's pink cameo brooch, someone else a flat-topped boater.

The café frequenters remind me of mating birds, bobbing across the ledge of a building, strutting tirelessly, singing with clear hearts so a mate will find them, so they can fly off into the island's high season, over unknown waters, which define the island. I visit the café in the mornings in case the ferry arrives. I wait for the narrative to begin. My narrative.

As a child, when riding on a bus, I'd pick out the other passengers who were marked to die before I could begin living, as though the bus were full of fractals on their way to separate but linked narratives. Narratives, too, have to wait their turn.

Some wait their whole lives for their narrative to begin.

Neither Acoma brother knew which parts of him were mortal or immortal, which parts were portals, which parts would live and which would die. They faced many dangers.

One danger is waiting for your narrative to appear secure enough to proceed. A terrible danger is the allure of safety.

The day I ordered a latte and mille-feuille, I had brought my copy of Rona's book, in case she came. She did. I thought she recognized me, but later realized that she walked over simply because of the book I was reading, her first one, the one she wrote when she still believed that searches could have an end, that the lost could be found. Her first book was full of faith in meaning. After its publication and she hadn't found her audience, she began to lose hope that she ever would. Each consecutive book was written in the belief that she herself was the lost one. Each book was summoned out of her need to refind herself. Each subsequent book was written by me in an attempt to locate Rona. When Rona would read her bound galleys right before publication, she'd feel certain that she wasn't the book's author, but she couldn't say who was. I had brought her first book with me, the only book that was completely her, the book that had sold two copies (one to me and the other to my mortal and immoral father).

Sometimes we have an infantile dependence on external conditions. Waiting for the right moment. A sign. Our need to read can be so great that it sometimes extends way beyond books; our need to read creates fictions everywhere—myths anywhere. Better to be illiterate.

Sitting beside my twin, holding her open book on my lap, bending language like blues flats drawn from a harp, I lied and said, "I need a spy for hire." Rona looked hungrily at my mille-feuille and asked if she could have a bite. I motioned *go for it* with my hand and watched her carefully lift a fork from another table, slice off a nice-sized piece, and shovel it into her mouth.

After appreciating the sweet, delicate tune, she said, "What's the intel you're after?"

"I'm after my twin."

I hated myself for this deception, but how else to get her to stay? There was some truth in my lie (as there often is). I couldn't fold my gangly arms around this stranger, this sister, and inform her that we were twins who had never met outside the womb. I'm not so nuts as to not realize that she'd think I was completely nuts. We were entering into a nonlinear dynamical system. Every student of literature knows that there is a variety of narrative models, such as the bildungsroman, romance, picaresque, and quest. Twin hunting usually takes the form of the quest. We were at the threshold— drinking coffee, eating French pastry, the air thick with smoke from opium.

A shadow figure materialized between Rona and me, wrapped itself around us like Spanish moss. I was consumed by a feeling of dread. Rona smiled as she watched the shadow slink into the cracks of my face, my wall— and her smile, like the sun, melted me. I beamed back…the wall fell. Test #1 of the quest was easily passed, though there was a moment when danger loomed and much was at stake. I barely recognized the critical moment. If it were not for the feeling of dread, I wouldn't have had an inkling of what had happened. How much does anyone ever have to lose? A question the gambler rarely asks. I have known a gambler or two in my life and have learned some of their tricks.

Knowledge is ephemeral and relative. It's valuable and changing.

"Mind your P's and Q's," my stepmother would scream at me. I thought she meant, *keep your nose clean*. I thought she meant, *pay attention to details*. I thought she meant, *mind your manners*. I never quite understood much of what Stepmother meant (mending and darning socks, damning and meaning only well). Many of Stepmother's meanings were attached to a lesson. She was a big proponent of quotations and clichés. Most of what my stepmother said contained very little context. So when Rona said to me, "What's the intel you're after?" my heart sank. I wanted to say, *You're the sister I saw while floating down the stream of our First Mother.* Though, of course, my words were the arms of my deception—they embraced and killed.

"Mind your P's and Q's," is what I said to Rona when she smiled at me and defeated the flesh-eating shadow. She winked and took another forkful of the mille-feuille, the cake of a thousand leaves.

Chapter 3

Once you've been found by loss, it will have its way with you whenever it wants; it won't let you go. At least that's how I see it.

One day I came home and my husband, Rene, was with a woman who looked exactly like me and spoke exactly like me and I was no longer me, exactly.

One of the hardest parts of loss is figuring out who you are in the glower of the seismic shift. After an immediate period of confusion, which felt like a brain contusion, I suffered a series of flashbacks that assured me my husband had always been this betraying man, and that at some point I had made an unconscious decision to be blind to it, to see him as a faithful, loyal man. "Loss" meant I had lost the thread of a story that I had made up—a fiction—and had been thrown into another story—a nonfiction—which I was not in control of. Loss became sulfuric, volcanic. Then loss became acceptance.

The cycle of loss began when I woke up for the first time and my twin was not by my side, an equivalent of the loss of the man who I believed was my best friend, who mutated into a cutting enemy, ripped from the role of soother, comforter, caretaker, from soul mate. Sun mate. Suddenly I was alone.

Nora (yup, third person again) would notice that on the day that intelligence had led to the capture of a murderous spy ring, she had caught a mouse in a spring trap. The time Rona interrogated a terrorist, Nora's cat, Whistler, gutted a bunny. How much did karma connect Nora and Rona?

Suddenly I felt alone.

I once had a wily Whistler who wanted *out* so badly that he tore through the screen door to escape the safe life that I had proudly provided. Home was too constricting for him.

Is sight or blindness more constricting?

Did I want him to stay or to follow his nose?

Whistler wanted to be cuddled and cared for, as well as to be lost in a forest of the moment, climbing an oak or stalking a deer. He wanted to fall asleep in a kaleidoscope of scents. He wanted simultaneously domestic bliss and reckless pleasures.

When Whistler shot through the door, my husband just about murdered me, as though he knew the projectile's trajectory was my dream, one as wild as Whistler's aerodynamic vault. The cat and I were red hot to blow that joint though feared even more the forest of our orphaned pasts. I might have left first, if I hadn't invested so much in the stronghold I'd created. I had constructed too many well-engineered walls to abandon them in order to hunt for bluebird eggs and chase rabbits or to dissect ferns that had shriveled up into question marks after the curtain of night fell. I had created a captor who followed me everywhere my mind could squeeze and was secretly deceiving me, devouring me, wittingly ripping my fragile wings, like Whistler did to breeding butterflies. Every story must have one element that the main character (the self) isn't aware of (a blind spot). Otherwise, how boring. In that particular tale, I signed up to be a blindsided Oedipus. I knew my husband's ways from the start and chose denial wisely in order for the family drama to be enacted.

So when I found Rona, it wasn't only thrilling that I found my twin, but also that a point of recurrence surfaced and I was allowed a momentary glimpse of assurance, a reminder that living is a process and no matter how lost and alone I might feel, I am not, that it's impossible to do this thing called *living* incorrectly, and just as impossible to do it perfectly. And just as impossible to do it alone.

"How can we be twins and have never seen the other's face?"

"There are many ways that could have happened."

Betrayal is part of my story. The man who betrayed me will return, only he might look different—he might even be Rona. He might be my lie to her.

Chapter 4

"How can we be twins and have never seen the other's face?"

"There are many ways that could have happened."

That, though, isn't what my twin asked me.

The first mirror dates back to way before the Bronze Age when glass is said to have been invented. Probably at the moment of consciousness, when man looked into still waters and saw himself, the mirror—along with the self and the other—originated. A toddler will notice the myriad mirrors hung throughout her home—step into each cool pool through her watery eyes—and enter a magical funhouse. When she's at a stage of development at which she understands she has individual desires and a personal path, the mirrors begin haunting her. She closes her eyes to play blind, to play peek-a-boo.

Together with the innovation of the mirror, our shadow side developed, a subtle distrust and denial, insidious as wandering veins in marble—one can't help but wonder if veins enhance beauty or mar the marble's uncontaminated consistency.

The first man-made mirrors were polished stone and/or metal. Later, glass was used in combination with mercury. Mercury poisons. Most interrogation rooms have one wall made from a double mirror. If it weren't for mirrors, we couldn't ever see ourselves, unless we were twins. After losing myself, I became determined to find my other.

What Rona asked me was: "When did you last see your twin?" She asked if I believed my twin was in danger. She asked for files and facts. I couldn't manage how to tell Rona what she wanted to know without distributing falsified and/or misleading information.

"How is a raven like a writing desk?"

Oedipus Rex collapses the various stages of life into one conundrum, one conundrum expands into a play viewed by an audience, actors performing to the fourth wall, spies reorganizing to build a fifth column— what walks on four legs, two legs, three? Boundaries erased by incest and the Sphinx's queries. Peek-a-boo.

Time collapsed cannot be counted, cannot be counted on.

"I will take your case," Rona assured me.

I exhaled a sigh of relief. "I'm going to find out who I am," I let escape.

"You sound like someone who's just about to start a search for self, not find a missing twin."

We walked to my house, which overlooks a calm body of water. My bedroom is built above the bay. I call it my subconscious room. The walls are cerulean and a crystal chandelier dangles from the ceiling. Sunlight bathes the room during the day and moon- or starlight bathes it at night. A father spirit protects it from Poseidon's wrath. The house is two stories; the two floors parallel one another. The first floor walls are lined with mirrors, so many mirrors that some who enter grow embarrassed. The top story is lined with books—novels and poetry. Story upon story upon song.

I can tell a lot about someone by the way they respond to my house. Some wrap their arms around themselves in an effort to protect a part that they are uncomfortable with. Some look down. Some remember as soon as they arrive that there was someplace they were supposed to be. Rona looked at the multitude of mirrors and the light, the waters outside rushing inside through the mirrors' reflections. And along with the flow of light and water was the rushing of Rona's deeper spirit. I'm sure she couldn't see how at home she was. "There is nothing so comfortable as your own safe skin," a sentry says in the play *Antigone.*

I made us iced tea and we sat beside a small aqua stream that runs through my living space, where I keep my collection of clementine koi.

(I am an amalgam of pasts, of plots.)

With ice cubes slapping her glass, which was foggy with chill, Rona explained, "A 'fetch' is a person's ghostly double. Some people have the talent to bi- or multilocate. It's not a mysterious phenomenon like astral projection. The subject is literally in more than one place; for instance, if I were here with you and simultaneously hiding under a folding chair in a conference room at the U.N., accumulating data."

"Can someone be more than one person? Can we have parallel missions to complete?"

"What's true for the fetch in one location is true in other locations." Rona leaned over. The orange light refracted off the koi and reflected on her cheek—a double color. Double sun.

Kittens are rarely twins but are fraternal multiples, each born in her own sac.

"I want you to help me find your twin. Will you do what I ask of you?" she said.

While I listened to her, I was aware of how truly familiar her scent was, that it set off an involuntary purr and activated my Jacobson's organ, my mouth ever so slightly open.

"And," she continued, "if I need you to go to two locations at the same time, would you try that, too?" She laughed. I laughed along, though I wasn't sure I understood the levity of the request.

"Watch your P's and Q's," I said.

Quests always require that we wake up and leave the house. Requests always require compromise. Some dangers are very close to home. Some are in our sleep, our dreams. Some never leave our minds. Some are in our beds. Sometimes by leaving our houses, we're saving our skin. Were my dangers lurking close or deep in the stage's wings? Was Whistler stalking to strike a vanishing monarch butterfly?

Rona was instructing me to leave my island.

Chapter 5

Taking the ferry to the mainland can't be compared to Odysseus's travels. The stretch of water isn't longer than ninety miles, and, still, it's a half day from shore to shore. Shallow waves rippling the water's brow, wondering what awaits on the other side. The other side of a coin, of a twin. Water mirroring sky. Water: my first mirror. The two orange range markers line up so the ferry won't run aground. Who can tell the depth of water from its surface? Water wears a poker face. It chills the air and leaves its passengers blinded.

When Oedipus returned to Thebes, he was hailed as a hero. He had no idea he had already killed his father. He had no idea of who he was, while he answered the riddle of who *we* are. The blinded passenger.

Someone once said, "To live is to defend a form," or something like that. I often think of that line first thing in the morning, when I'm still jellylike. Will I defend the form today? Fight the good fight? Or will I return to the ocean, to one undifferentiated dream?

The usefulness of determining and anticipating changing behavior and/or beliefs was the backbone of my card game. Artificial intelligence. And although how one plays does matter with respect to our daily quality of life, whether we die feeling that we have lived purposeful or useless lives matters little in the end. Both ways, we've served an unknown purpose. The grand gestures have to do with our ancestors, butterflies in Indiana, ghosts that move furniture. Even Whistler was subject to strict rules that appear arbitrary in our blind state.

The water has always been friendly to me. The holy water. When I was one and learning to walk, I accidentally stumbled into a swimming pool and the water carried my limbs aloft on its back. My stepmother, seeing my predicament, dove in, and when she bored into the water, its salty buoyancy assaulted her. It behaved not at all like a swimming pool, but like the Dead Sea. Water defended the form, defeated form, defined "transform." Formless water. From then on, it was my gal pal. When frightened today, I remember that blood is 83% water, that I'm floating always. So as I journeyed on the ferry with my twin to face my fate, I relied on my faith in water to carry me. And a story:

The evil stepmother wanted to be rid of her husband's twin children, so she sent them into the forest to care for an old, dusty woman who she conveniently hadn't mentioned was a witch who feasted on sweet morsels of children. On the way to the witch, the children detoured to visit their own grandmother, their own flesh and blood, their own dharma sister. (The forest is filled with the elderly—each cottage stores an old woman with warts, wise words, or wands of witch hazel switches, a forest of widows, a forest of women. The forest as an elderly facility.) The kids' granny outed the stinky hag and, handing them bread, milk, and ham, told them to be civil, to never touch a crumb that was offered (words to adhere to when visiting foreigners' homes), and to always watch their hands, wash their hands. Once at the witch's place, the twins bribed wrens, a cat, mice, and a mangy mutt with their bread, milk, and ham, and the animals showed the children a magic route out of their shame, where witches cannot comb. The cat in particular was helpful, which pissed off the witch because the cat was her familiar.

"You Benedict Arnold," the wishy-washy witch squeaked.

"Never a meatless bone out of you, while the twins toss me whole ham hocks" was the bony cat's snub.

I thought of my stepmother diving into the swimming pool to save me. I thought of her dressing us in Mommy and Me matching outfits, her Chinese face and my Caucasian one beaming at strangers, who'd comment, "Like mother, like daughter." My stepmother died last year. Some children in fairy tales have a guardian angel that monitors their lives, "watches over them." I like to imagine my stepmother as my fairy godmother. She tells me where witches are hiding. She advises me to be civil (mind your P's and Q's) and to always bring bread, milk, and ham when traveling to unknown lands. My stepmother was far from perfect. She could be too Confucian; nevertheless, I feel her diving through my 83% watery blood to protect me.

I look over at Rona as we're nearing land and become aware that she's a double agent and therefore not to be trusted. A moment of clarity? I see her as a fractal. I see a shape forming in the distance that is a whole. The wren advised: plug up the holes of the sieve with clay before transporting water. The wren warned that the twin was being set up. The twin listened, did what she was told. The wren ate breadcrumbs from the twin's hand. My stepmother said, "Don't eat strange food." My stepmother said, "Water reflects one's heart and soul." My stepmother taught me to raise koi, to always ask for help from wrens.

Chapter 6

The governing Board of Trustees is convening. It is my job to recognize—from the many whom I've come in contact with—which are members in a closed session and which are fellow drifters. In my knapsack, I carry bread, milk, and ham in case an animal (guard or guide) needs bribing.

Rona and I stood shoulder to shoulder as the ferry pulled into port. We reflected on our reflections in the glassy sea. A portly woman, starboard from us, in Landlubber jeans was reading *The Thorn Birds*, which I recognized as the 1977 best-selling novel.

"What's she doing here?" I asked Rona.

"Tonight's the Night," my sister replied.

I took out my iPhone and snapped Ms. Landlubber just in case she was a time aberration who popped in from the year Rod Stewart had a *Billboard* hit and flare-bottoms were the rage. The meeting had begun, though the agenda was unknown by me—life was regathering from "all time/all place," a harmonic convergence of "me" fields or "we" fields in search of one another through intuition/initiation/imagination. I had no notion of whether the Board of Trustees, the Corporation and Signatories, was here to harm me. Or even if Rona was a plant. I thought of Rene, my ex, and watched my hands. This was the first time in a long time that I was visiting the mainland. I believed I'd been sent to cater to the needs of a witch. I believed my twin and I were in search of the other, that we were in search of the self. I wished Whistler were here, my bonny cat who flew screaming through a screen door and ended up lassoed into heaven by a feline god.

"Mortals are immortals and immortals are mortals; the one living the other's death and dying the other's life," Heraclitus wrote. The twins with different fathers, one mortal, one immortal, the bilocaters who exhibit on different frequencies.

I do have a sister whom I grew up with. Okay, she's a stepsister, but still just as real as a sister could be, just as my stepmother could well have been my "real" mother, except that she was Chinese and I was born in another's womb. Yes, there is a relative life that I'm bound to, a life, unlike the absolute one, that doesn't include Rona, a life with P's and Q's, with regular Sunday phone calls back home, with axioms my stepmother pounded into me, a true life. And then there is the *other* one. The life that pulls me toward timelessness, toward isinglass, which my shadow self uses as a window to peer through universal time. Riverine. Runny flying sunny.

One father was mortal and one was immortal. A clue.

Whistler was blue like Vishnu.

"Are you a wren?"

My favorite Dr. Seuss was *Are You My Mother?* I identified with the crazy bird who had no idea where she came from but was open to investigation.

Before my waters were filled with clementine koi, I owned a Siamese fighting fish. Because he had to be in a tank by himself, I gave him a mirror, a castle, and a bamboo tree (ego, superego, and id). I also gave him a name—Superfish! Superfish was the star of a superhero narrative. And like all superheroes, he had one fatal weakness—he was incapable of breathing air. With a mirror, castle, and bamboo tree, his life was perfect. In the mornings, I'd lovingly watch Superfish snore, splayed out on the upper bamboo branches much like a wild chicken (who also enjoys a good snooze in a tree). I'd imagine he was dreaming of saving schools of fish, if only he didn't have to live his life in seclusion because his superpowers induced him to tear to smithereens any sole that swam in his path. So, I imagined that he passed his life in his fortress of solitude, dreaming of what he'd do if only he were more typical.

Then, one atypical morning, I passed Superfish's tank on my way to the toilet and lo and behold, the mirror reflected no fish in cerulean water:

the castle had been evacuated. On the floor, beneath the tank, was a dessicated, dehydrated Superfish. I could only surmise what had happened. I imagined Superfish attempting to sleep atop his famed tree, which had rootlessly risen to the water's surface. Superfish leapt out of the water to roost, but instead faced his deadly foe, his original fear/his original face. Every superhero has enemies and a secret identity. Every superhero has a fatal weakness. Every superhero has a superego. My Superfish dove from his mortal body and into his dream, where he dozes today.

Chapter 7

I dove from my island onto the mainland. Rona by my side. Rona on my back. The Watchers and the Corporation in the wings.

My father was a stevedore, the most handsome man at the dock. He wore a metaphoric fedora. My father knew how to be cruel. How to be kind. How to be cute. The tallest man at the port, one foot in water, one on land. His foamy fears moving and smoothing and shaping the stepping-stones he planted on his shore. My father whistling a melody that secreted exotic tales, dark uncharted depths. My father who had fathered many females on the island and equipped us with monster-fighting gear, ready to slay demon (da men) wherever we go. My father ate his boys at the moment of conception. He spat them out onto the earth to plant races of men; he spat them into the air to seed planets. There is no greater one than my father, my father who destroys and creates.

At the dock, there was Father, driving the straddles. When he saw me, he began the long process of lowering his beginningless and endless crane. He always gravitated toward the challenges of the waterfront. I was sure he had died. Stories of his suicide have filled history books. Children study his death in school as readily as they study his mariner's poetry. While rowing toward god, he gassed himself. Once when I was in the café, a nightbird came up to me and said she had seen him recently at the dock. I said he's dead. She said she had thought so, too, but apparently he isn't. I nodded my head, as though I believed her. "Isn't that nice," I said, though I thought she was a lunatic.

"Daddy, it *is* you."

He kissed me and told me he had missed seeing me so much that he convinced the Watchers to let him slip through the flimsy fabric that separates the worlds.

"So, you're back." I pronounced what seemed obvious as I hugged him. His skeletal body lacked warmth and appeared oddly transparent.

Let me tell you about leaving:

An emerald leaf with a million diamond facets.

Mille-feuille, a cake of a thousand leaves.

Taking my leave.

My liege.

My leave of absence.

Following a long, sinewy path.

It is fall and leaves bruise and die—they fall to the hardening arteries that cover the earth. It's a cold fall and I climb trees to reach for apples—gold and red—the colors of memory leaves, dying, leaving.

Leaving can be seen as red. A bruise caused by love, my fatal weakness.

When I was in fourth grade, I became obsessed with autumn leaves. I'd collect bagfuls of ones that were my favorite colors and pin them under glass like butterflies with bright, fragile wings. I'd let them loose in my room, a fan blowing them through airstreams and dreams. I'd shine lights into them to see their blood. I'd cover my crisp white sheets with crisp bright leaves and sleep soundly on their heckling hiccups.

Stepmother would scream that I was bringing death and winter into her house. She'd get the broom and start sweeping. Sweeping. Sweeping. In her sleep, her hands—two balls clutching a dream broomstick and miming a sweeping motion—sweeping. When my stepmother would think I was out of earshot, I'd hear her sing Chinese prayers to plead for pity on her useless daughter who could never understand the ways of the world. (Stepmother would often go on about the ways of the world, as though they were written in a book from which some could read, while others—such as myself—were forever excluded.)

I try to imagine my father and stepmother when they were young, that instant when their ways of the world collided. My stepmother and father swaying, sweeping toward one another, weeping away from the other. Their encounter must have been that brief, now deeply buried in their past, in my bones. No language exists that can speak of it. A palimpsest in a dead and forgotten tongue.

"Don't bring winter into the house!"

I see my father, vibrant red and gold, the hues of autumn leaves, who, alive again, connived death. My stepmother, soft whites shaded by blues and greens, my foreign mother who would have given her life for me, my good-dream mother. I peer over at Rona, Rona the spy who doesn't know what side she's on.

"Rona," I say, "this man could be your father. He is the right age. His eyes resemble yours."

Rona says she hasn't seen her father in years. Or rather, there is a man that her mother tells her is her father, the man her mother sleeps with, but he's not the same man who was her father when she was growing up. "And isn't that when someone is your father?" she asks. "When you're growing up?"

Yes, she believes the stevedore could be her father, this poet who mans a crane, who wears his enmity like the tattoo on his shoulder.

A leaf with a million emerald facets.

A forest with a million emerald leaves.

Mille-feuille, a cake of a thousand leaves.

A blade of glass.

My liege.

A leaf of absence.

Ingredients

3 puff pastries

500 g caster sugar

1 dozen egg yolks

1 vanilla pod

2 shots kirsch

Icing sugar for dusting

Ingredients

1 small woman (pretty, kind)

2 men, one bright, the other a wild card (possibly reckless)

1 rectangular home with an apple tree outside the window (cut in small squares)

Dust and ice

Ingredients

A library of old books

Hemp rope

Leave out to rest for the rest of the night.

Chill.

Whisk until well blended.

I have a suspicion that the stevedore who looks like my father is a fetch, that my real father is someplace else, always somewhere that I'm not.

I first met my husband at a party. I ran up to him when he walked through the door and I cut a red slice from his cheek, a lasting kiss. Years later, when he heard me relay the story of how I branded him at first sight, he offered up an alternative tale. "We were at a party," he said, "but you didn't talk. You haunted the perimeter of the room and watched while I mingled with others." Finally he asked our mutual friend who I was and why I maintained my distance. "A bird of prey or a timid lemur?"

"A wild cat," our friend said.

My ex believed her, and from then on he felt most comfortable with me in the woods and at business parties, convinced I'd protect him from beasts that feed on fresh flesh.

Our "love at first sight" is an amalgam of beliefs and folktales. I'm convinced that we had not been in the same space for our first several rendezvous, and from the moment we did join worlds, we started slowly leaving one another.

This is a book about leaving, yet some unique species never do. Seychelles warblers often remain in their parents' nests rather than leave to raise families of their own. Some stay, no matter how painful a situation becomes, no matter what must be sacrificed.

I never wanted to leave the island. I have often wondered if choices that I've made were predicated on staying, whatever the cost. Oedipus's downfall wasn't that he slept with his mother and killed his father, but that he tried to change his destiny, that he wouldn't accept the fate that the gods assigned him.

Did I end up marrying my father and then taking leave of my senses? Making up a story about having a twin? And these Watchers, this water, are they here to guide me to another shore? Are we all on our way?

I put my arm around my sister to keep her close.

She nods. I nod. We close our eyes.

Since meeting Rona, I have seen my limitations. I have faced my rapacious denial.

The French psychiatrist Pierre Janet coined the term "splitting" to refer to a useful defense mechanism: fragmenting oneself as a way of facing trauma. Anna Freud, a spitting image of her father, further investigated the phenomenon and considered it a "natural" developmental stage, not a psychosis, which is how most mind sorcerers had seen it before her.

Splitting.

Bilocating.

Facing a mirror.

How many selves self-reproduce in the environment of one body? How many cells in a lifetime? How many prisms reflect how many us(es)— or our uses?

How do we look at that which is most horrifying? Our single face?

My stepmother took particular pleasure in telling me how useless I was. For her, there was no more disagreeable trait than uselessness. When she was "fit to be tied," she'd evoke Confucius, who said:

"It does not matter how slowly you go

So long as you do not stop."

I'd scream back Tao Te Ching's:

"Thirty spokes share the wheel's hub;

It is the center hole that makes it useful.

Shape clay into a vessel;

It is the space within that makes it useful.

Cut doors and windows for a room;

It is the holes that make them useful.

Therefore, profit comes from what is there;

Usefulness from what is not."

According to the Tao, there's a usefulness in uselessness.

In the realm of trees. In the realm of females (or "remales" as Stepmother would often say). No hollow bird bone of contention between Stepmother and me on this point!

Rona tells me her favorite story, which is about twin murderers:
"A twin (twin #2) murders a husband. The husband was a real animal who would claw and ravage the wife (twin #1). Once he was dead, the other twin (2) properly stuffed him with ashes and insects. When the wife (1) saw her husband, she took him for alive and beat him with a stick. He burst open and the wife (1) was molested by his inner insects/instincts (stinks).

"The wife (1) was in possession of a ball of twine that was large enough to measure the world.

"The twin (2) carried away the wife (1) to feed her to ants. To try to escape the ants, the wife (1) jumped into the river. Grandmother told Deer—

Grandmother's husband—that the woman (1) she found floating in the river had given birth to two lovely twins (twins #3 and #4). Those twins (3 and 4) came out of the cradle to play with Grandfather Deer while Grandmother went into the forest to fetch Deer some fresh tortillas.

"Bird warned Deer.

"Bird warned Grandmother.

"Cat warned twins.

"The Watchers (Bird and Cat) decided to meet to discuss a suitable punishment for the notorious murdering twin (2). Impulsive Cat was unable to behave himself and had a field day with Bird, a day in the field with flittering Bird flying for its life."

Things happen as they happen, no matter how much anyone knows.

No matter who is warned.

"Grandmother returned once Bird fell asleep.

"Twins (1 and 2) turned into Sun and Moon and drove Grandmother out of her house, morning and night.

"Deer was filled with wasps. Bad dreams. Deer's tongue was stung, swollen. He learned his lesson. Woke up. Forgot his lesson. Forgot his death. Forgot he got a sharp tongue-lashing."

Twins turn into mothers, fill with babies. Twinning.

The ball of twine unwinds in the winds and space is finally measured—only thing is that for each being (human, animal, plant) the measurement varies, ever so slightly.

Why?

(This is the riddle that must be answered.)

Rona is a zoomorphic sphinx—she's a lion with a human head; she's "the strangler," triangular. A stranger to herself. A murdering twin to a husband/wife/grandmother/deer. She's the liar, one of four big cats. Lionesses hunt for their pride. Over 4,000 years ago, cats were domesticated by Egyptians who worshiped felines. The domestication process must have been slow, painful, loving. Rona is part of that process. I am, too. We are standing on the mainland, holding hands. Somewhere miles away, there are two others of us, holding hands, knowing. And another two on a different mainland, maybe in a different time. At this moment, it becomes clear. Multilocating fetches and dreams and travelers meeting at a harmonic crossroads of understanding. Zoomorphic (shapeshifting into animal). Octants (eight parts of a three-dimensional Euclidian coordinate system).

My father interrupts the moment and calls out, "Daughter." Rona and I turn to face him. *There is still time to work out our relationship before he dies*, I think. I see him growing lighter while I'm thinking that he's not yet dead. *Still time.* "I'll get my things," Rona calls back to him. If I weren't watching this scene, if I were listening to it—over a shortwave radio, let's say—I would believe that I was witnessing the most unextraordinary interaction. Father calling daughter, daughter packing up things to join father. And yet, nothing looks right. Father is fading, daughter is packing light (literally) and molecules of smoke. And they are running off together, to someplace I can't fathom. And they are taking something of me with them and leaving something of them with me. No, nothing that is happening is typical, of that I am sure. And at this moment I suspect that I'm pregnant and following a long sinewy path:

It's a winding way. Windblown snow obfuscates. Bright-winged birds tender color, feathers gingerly falling across the lacy surface of water. It is no longer fall, and rose and honey colors have followed a separate path. Where the earth and sea are bristling and fallow, I am trudging.

Chapter 8

What I remember about First Mother are her cinnamon walls, like the impenetrable, unexplainable ones that guard the palace rooms of the Forbidden City, the ones where my future was stored. Obsidian, onyx, petrified ebony. A body of dark stone from distant planets. A "me" that was forming, had formed, was dying, a no-form/formless me, a "me" with fins, a tail, an ancient "me" that wasn't yet, in a mother who was and yet wasn't. There was a reed basket. It appeared from moment to moment on a riverbank that blew melodies, warm and legato, flowing through me; I grew while traveling down her silvery stream. Every moment, pregnant with variation and possibility, curled within the interior courtyard of Mother #1, who wanted me badly until she saw my needy body and my raspberry face, always crying my *fucken head off.* "Shut your trap!" she'd outscream my ear-splitting squeals. The first world was resonant with sirens and howls, deep bowels and singing bowls. When I think of that mother, I try to remember how good she was inside and how well her body cared for me.

Inside the island of Mother, I first met my shadow. A second self. A sister. Before one can discern who one is, the entire body and mind that existed in one moment has been transformed in the next. Examining the water of self is like probing the changing tide. When I was inside First Mother, I'd hear a sound without wondering where it came from. The sound wasn't linked to reference—there were no memories. I would hear a bell, and then I wouldn't. Moment by moment.

Even my sense of being a doppelganger was not yet developed; it was a sixth sense yet to form. I have heard that Narcissus couldn't distinguish self from mirror image, but I have always believed that he, too, was born with a twin who disappeared at the moment of birth, and that what he pined for was not himself, but the other. Just as every moment is born and dies. Like every twin is there, and not, both depressed and dressed alike and hunted together in an ancient myth, moving into the present. Thanatos—Death—had influence over humans, while his twin—Hypnos—held sway over gods. One mortal, one immortal. Who could tell which was which? Where silent and twilight shadows reign, empty dream-shapes mimic form.

Rona was a big cat, even then, even there, a *Panthera*. Sometimes, as a nonformed formless form, I'd follow her through the badlands of Mother #1, the gullies and canyons eroded by wind and water. Little sister chasing the echo of her twin. Following her to shore.

"I'm after my twin," I said.

That was the first home, the first island, the first ferry I took through the First Mother's channel.

"Huzzah," Rona said.

A fanfare on this side of the coast.

There are sequences that get established. Once established, it's hard to break free. Like some relationships. Like some feelings. Patterns of behavior. Lace patterns. Patterns of china. The blue willow. The wayfarer. The prodigal son. Now that I was on the mainland and Rona had disappeared with my father the stevedore, and I was alone, I decided to seek out my ex and Whistler.

But where to find them?

Nora (I'm falling, falling into third person point of view) picked up *To the Lighthouse*—which had been packed in an oversized shoulder bag—partly because she had two feet on the mainland and her mind, which had a mind of its own, wanted to turn into sea and partly because she knew that the DNA of her past lay in the frame of mind she inhabited when her senses were filled with specters, their scents and stories. She'd mumble the words of long-gone Virginia Woolf, as Woolf wrote them in 1925, imagining the melding of her and Woolf's mouths, and Nora thought back to that very unspectacular day years before, when, waiting to hear the results of her biopsy, she was reading an old paperback edition of the novel and felt a subtle change. A new, unsubstantial memory took hold as sometimes happens when a dreamer sees the person who had been dreamed, and the dreamed one, who had shared the intimacy of a dream, no longer behaves as unselfconsciously as he had before the dream, as though he knows how deeply he entered the dreamer in the night when the two became one, colluding, now blushing when each sees the other trying hard not to look— the dream, dreamer, and dreamed, a complicit, completed, complicated painting like Lily Briscoe's in the dream novel that Virginia Woolf scribed. Only it is impossible not to look. Only it is impossible not to want the cancer a little. Only then could Nora become who she had once believed she was, on that last day that she remembered herself as being only Nora. Now, looking for her ex and her oracle cat, she read the thoughts of Woolf's presiding artist, Lily, who painted destinies:

"What art was there, known to love or cunning, by which one pressed through into those secret chambers? What device for becoming, like waters poured into one jar, inextricably the same, one with the object one adored? Could the body achieve, or the mind, subtly mingling in the intricate passages of the brain? or the heart? Could loving, as people call it, make her and Mrs. Ramsey one? For it was not knowledge but unity that she desired, not inscriptions on tablets, nothing that could be written to men, but intimacy itself, which is knowledge, she had thought, leaning her head on Mrs. Ramsey's knee."

I looked up and Whistler was resting his hard blue china chin on my knee. His eyes and mouth open ever so slightly and his soothing purr vibrating from my thigh into my heart. Could loving make us one?

The night Whistler died, a gray cat followed me into a valley, through a green meadow, up to the restoring hill, as I traveled brushland, attempting to escape company. Whistler had sent a stubborn companion to shadow me. The night Whistler died, a mangy-looking cat slept by my feet, guarding my dreams. Whistler died on Good Friday. Whistler died in a moment. Continuity ended for me after Whistler's death. My stepmother's death was protracted. I saw her senselessly suffer. I watched her drown in her own fluids. Our bodies make no sense. They cheat us, cheat on us. They are unfaithful and abandoning.

The life that's growing in my womb, the cells madly reproducing, taking nutrients from me, stealing thoughts from me, lifting my dreams, the life that is taking mine, cancer or pregnancy?

I visited the Valley of Death after Whistler was taken from me and I wouldn't let him go, and he wouldn't let me go, either. Both of us on our last walk, respectively. That night, he was the mangy stranger at my feet, and in his unconscious, I was a final shape that he rested beside, a shore that was traveling away from him.

I closed *To the Lighthouse.* Children die in every book.

Chapter 9

There are numerous curio and memento shops by the mainland docks. They are filled with self-exiles and tourists who speak private languages and travel alone, who sleepwalk down labyrinthine aisles with cheap souvenirs. Humans out of context, rummaging through trinkets. The woman behind the counter, the woman who tends the register, has silver plaited hair and emerald eyes that are tinged with burgundy and gold. She's from a northern country and has seen the aurora borealis—an ionic glow that, when brushed onto the night sky, produces a greenish blush.

The woman behind the counter observes the exiles as they make their revolutions around her store. Occasionally one will admire a thimble or a palm-sized plate, useless objects whose sole purpose is to be picked up and turned over, a warehouse of generic memories. When the price tag can't be found, the exile will look at an identical one for a clue to the cost. The traveler could not know that at this store there are no set prices. Not confident of his English, he holds up the trinket and spits out, "Want." The woman behind the counter stares into his eyes and shudders. She sees all that the tourist has given up to get here. His sick mother requested he remain at home, but his trip had been planned for a year and he didn't believe that when he returned to his place of birth anything would be different. It never was, exactly what he hated about where he was from. There, change was doled out only by cashiers and could be viewed only in cold, dark movie theaters. His mother, who always complained too loudly, embarrassed him before his friends. The neighbors imitated her behind her back, though, unfortunately, not behind his.

When he returns to Brugge, she will no longer be living. His little sister will be under his care for the next five years, until she is eighteen, and she marries the first stranger who will allow her to escape her brother's desolation and guilt. The traveler will spend the rest of his life regretting that he abandoned his mother to visit trinket stores in a handful of distant cities. At the same time, he will be aware that his life will have changed for the better because of his decision to go; hence, the question which haunts him: Were his travels the key to freedom or a staunch shackle to regret? The moment of his death will give him the answer.

The woman behind the counter asks for a dollar. "You've paid a lot to get here," she says to him as she carefully wraps the fragile souvenir in tissue paper. "Go home now; maybe you'll return in time."

The traveler looks into the cashier's windowed eyes and at her winsome smile and imagines he misunderstands her. "Go home now; maybe you'll return in time" must be an American idiom that means "Enjoy your trip." He is surprised by the price of the trinket. He has seen it sold in other stores and knows it goes for ten dollars elsewhere. *I really got a deal,* he thinks. *The gods are watching over me.* A customer on line behind the man from Brugge hands the cashier the same exact trinket, but from this cavalier gentleman she asks for twenty dollars.

"Humph!" he yells at the witchy woman as he retuns the junk to the shelf and storms out the door.

The woman behind the cash register tallies stars and karmic debt. She evens out scores. Most conversations and exchanges are finalized with a word or short phrase—"How much?" or "A dollar," or "Please." That's it, though the amount said in those few syllables is vast and haunting.

"Who was that young man?" I ask the cashier.

She is surprised that I understand she's a sorceress. "Some pay dearly for very little," she replies.

"Am I paying too much for what I want?"

The soft perambulations of sleepwalking customers, each an island unto himself. Looking. Looking for the unique object that they can afford, that will draw them home and place them here, the object that straddles two worlds.

The silvery witch eyes me. I imagine she's deciding what to reveal. She reaches under the counter and hands me a pair of cowrie shells.

"How much for these?" I ask.

"I'm paying you."

Before I can say more, she calls out, "Next!" to a small girl, who hands her a milky porcelain key with blue sailboats painted on the glaze. I recognize my face in the girl. My almond eyes, only younger. A softer version of my pointy chin.

"How much?" the girl asks. I see the father waiting at the store's portal. A foghorn blows in the distance. The girl and man are clearly kin. I see my father in the man. My handsome father. My arrogant father looking sweetly at this young child who's paying for something by herself for the first time. Did he once look at me that way, with his own youthful pride, many years ago?

The cashier's eyes water as she softly says, "Take it."

I want to know what she sees in the future for the child, what she sees for me. The girl leaps with joy. She has done it—she has bought a present and paid the right price. She runs swiftly into her dad's arms. I'm in my dad's arms. Such pleasure and sorrow surround the shores of this store that's bodysurfing the edge of sleep and wakefulness. Dreams being realized and reality lighting the surface, while rooted in the source, the deepest part of the ocean. Terrible missteps and wind gliding with the energy of time, different from what was and will be.

I place the cowrie shells in my pocket, the trinkets that I've paid for with my life. The Romans called cowries "porculi" or "little pigs," a term that developed into "porceletta." The word "porcelain" was coined by Europeans to describe the cowrielike finish seen on Far Eastern pottery. Cowrie is a fertility symbol and a magical trademark for prosperity—used for money in China and as protection from the African oceanic goddess. The shells are the mouth of the orisha (multidimensional spirits that reflect the Creator). I can throw them back into the ocean along with flowers and honey, the ocean that absorbs into it all creation, while creation transforms into ocean. The ocean becoming its parts/parts becoming ocean. The light and sound become you. Sounds and screams of *becoming* fill the air. I can know this, but I cannot see it. I am given two cowrie shells by a santera but have no gift of divination. I am given life but have no innate sense of gratitude. I can throw the shells into the ocean as an offering, to show that I have *learned* to be grateful. I can throw myself into the ocean to be embraced. My heart can open and flood with blood.

I can. But I don't. I sit on the dock with my shells and place one in each hand. There is so little that I understand. I hear the music of foreign languages, calls of birds, the barking dog. Tidings from the tongue, none of it I get. The Tower of Babel. I place one cowrie against each ovary. Cancer or birth? What grows there/here? Soon I will be dead or a twin of a new sort—a mother. *A bird sat on her egg. "I must get something for her to eat," she said. So away she went.* My father has gone off with Rona; Rona has taken him away. Grief forms in waves. It mounts and passes. I hear the foghorn again. The distance is disappearing. Froth. Backwash.

Chapter 10

The scientist, whose lifework was to study fog, had died. The scientist who spent his life exploring the field of fog. Who dedicated his life to the study of fog. As a student, he could not have foreseen that he would specialize in fog. That he would shine a fresh light on the study of fog. As a fogologist. Eulogies were given by his esteemed colleagues in the Department of Fog on the cloudy day that he was buried. The words "fog" and "God" were invoked and substituted for one another effortlessly, as often occurs on the commonplace yet momentous occasion of one's death. The study of fog was greatly advanced because of his insights.

He would have his assistant sweep sunshine off the laboratory deck for hours, until time could not be counted. Sweeping away sunshine. Invoking the invisibility of dew, moisture, fog. The assistant's balled-up fists clutching a broomstick, sweeping, sweeping. She'd tiptoe up to the window of the high-tech hole-in-the-wall, foglike, and spy on the scientist, fogging up the window with her breath. The liquid assistant would dream of fog. Every morning she'd plan on quitting her low-paying job, but upon seeing the slow-crawling fog drag itself over her mysterious lake, she'd suit up as if a prisoner of some purpose she couldn't understand, reach for her grayish khakis, float into them and then out the door to work. Fog is fog—not moisture, not cloud.

It is adorned with no solid form.

Since fog is adorned with no solid form, fog is adorned with the fog's no solid form. Fog is the killing of fog adorned with no solid form. Therefore, fog is fog as fog and fog is not fog as fog.

And sunshine can be swept and swept for hours and still leave some stain of light, morning until night, adorning the form of liquid wood, which is trees, which is fungus, which is worms, which is fog.

The day the stevedore appeared at the lab was most unusual. First off, that day there was no fog creeping over Mu Qing's lake, so after opening an eye that morning and peering out her window, she quickly closed it and fell back into a deep, deep sleep. A forest sleep. When she awoke several hours later and arrived several hours late for work, she expected her boss, who was lead scientist in the study of fog, to upbraid her, but he did no such thing. Instead, he complimented her on her clothes, not the grayish work pants she always wore with a white lab coat, not the blue that she'd wear when she wasn't dressed for work, but an emerald frock the color of gleaming seaweed.

The stevedore was a danger from the moment her boss introduced them. *He is the fog*, she thought, *crawling over the lake to come to me. He is the fog, beckoning me to follow.*

My stepmother never feigned innocence about my father. She understood what he was from the moment he followed her up the stairs to her top floor.

"And he disappeared like fog," she said to me.

I had many questions for her about the day the fog skipped her lake and entered her life, but because of the precision of the way that she relayed the story—the formulation of it, really—I was unable to voice them. Mu Qing addressed me as a scientist offering a student an equation to be memorized, not as a mother telling her daughter how she met her father.

"And he disappeared like fog."

Once Stepmother started seeing the stevedore, he would appear to her at odd hours and with unique and thoughtful gifts. During one of his typically irregular visits, he brought *me*.

"My daughter," he said, placing me in the crux of my stepmother's willowy arm.

Mu Qing rubbed the soft spot on the top of my head and was delighted as I beamed back at her. Stepmother says my beacon of light shone on her first, before anyone else. Of course, my stepmother could not have known such a thing; nevertheless, her version of the incident has become a family myth. The other myth regarding my arrival is that my father found me in a reed basket by a stream with a giant blue cat protector. The story goes that the cat hissed at every passerby who'd come near, except for Father. When he approached, the cat opened his mouth ever so slightly, to activate his Jacobson's organ, and immediately abandoned his watch, leaping into the forest.

My stepmother quit the lab soon after she began raising me, but when the scientist died, she threw flowers and honey into the ocean, and she howled in the wind. What can I say?

It's the only story I've been told about my birth,

told to me by my stepmother, who was magnetized by fog, who is fog

not moisture, not cloud

adorned with no solid form

since fog is adorned with no solid form; therefore, fog is adorned with the fog's no solid form. Fog is the killing of fog adorned with no solid form. Fog is the form of fog adorned with no solid form. Therefore, fog is fog as fog and fog is not fog as fog.

Chapter 11

"Shiva has three eyes that are always open. The ocean whispers its sonnets into his conch shell ear while he partakes of the fluid god's poisons and spicy perfumes. He sits on a tigress's back when he travels the land.

"Vishnu or universal/unreal/feral essence—beyond past, beyond future. The divine color, dark blue clouds of form/nonform, creates and destroys outside space/time.

"Shiva and Vishnu traverse the parallelogram of life together. They take numerous forms, cross various fluids and seas and the bodies that ride them. As teachers, they challenge us; as intimates, they amuse us. We pass them in fields throughout our lives, in color-field paintings, in fallow fields, cornfields, in vector fields, akashic fields, in snowy fields.

"Odysseus came upon the two Hindu gods in the forms of Scylla and Charybdis at the Strait of Messina. Scylla, a monster of the ocean caves, and her fraternal twin, Charybdis, the belching whirlpool dragon. Avoiding one meant falling prey to the other. Scylla (Vishnu, the destroyer) ate sailors and Charybdis (Shiva) sucked up water and spit out whirlpools. Odysseus placed his bet on Vishnu, sacrificing a few to save his ship."

I tell this story to the young girl who bought the porcelain key with the sailboat design. She wants passage into the door of adulthood even though she's only three feet, five inches. She sits on my lap and asks to be told adventures of the high seas. I consider constructing a yarn about a girl pirate who steals doubloons, a Pippi Longstocking sailor type who walks the plank blindfolded and sword fights her way through the angry open ocean. But regrettably, I detail a morality tale that advocates sensible behavior. Warnings. Lessons. I've become Mu Qing.

The girl's father calls her and she runs to him, an established pattern of response, running toward voices—the call of her father, her future boyfriends and girlfriends, her talents—forms of rarified ocean. She has the china key to open doors and runs naturally toward sound. She will never know this about herself. She cannot and will not ever be able to say no to sound. I should tell her the tale of the Sirens, but her father's calling, and there's no stopping her—she must run.

I sit at the shore with the cowries, one shiny skull resting in the palm of each hand, a snail's back on which universes balance, the precarious fate of sentient life carrying me through warm seas. I see a turtle. I see breaking waves.

Always forming/reforming/uniforming/uninforming. How do we measure oscillating liquid? Answering the Sphinx's riddle was part of Oedipus's fate, not a shield from it. "Who am I?" is what he wanted to know. And when he found out, he blinded himself so that seeing his face would never bias his insight. No matter what distance we remain from the looking glass, it is always halfway between our bodies and our projections, in a virtual reality that lives inside the mirror. Our captured soul in the mirror is always half our size. It's always a discrete space for our material as well as our projected selves. The glass wall that stands in the way of seeing, being. An iconoclast smashes it (us). Replacements wait on the sidelines. Space opens for the fetch that multilocates. Shards of glass reflecting incidental light, so real and such a remarkable falsity, like dreams, like desires, like our life in this realm (samsara). So many delusions of painted scenery, towns, stage managers, incidents captured like light, like shadow, incipient ambient light, parabolic.

I wanted to return to the store, to the shore, to return the cowries when the thought arose that they are my "bank," that after the game ends, the facedown cowries will conceal the winning or losing numbers. I had received a karmic boon from a stranger. I could return or keep the cowries. I could place them in a vase like the gifts that Rene used to leave for me, flowers arranged in a vase and placed by my bedside, sweet-scented flowers to help me follow dreams, dream flowers.

The day after I left the home that my husband and I had built together, Rene invited my replacement to move into our bedroom, presented her with a charm bracelet that he had bought for me, diminutive birds—wren, finch, warbler—cast in silver and chained together.

Rene's lover sensed me in the shiny birds and pushed them away.

"It's not my style," she said. "I'm no fool," she said.

She wasn't compliant like me. She fought. Refused. She stated her opinions, tastes. She demanded her desires be met. The moment that he moved her into our house, she commenced redecorating, then renovating, then demolishing. Even after the house was razed, she declared they were moving—she wouldn't live in my shadow, in my light, on property where I'd be bilocating, staring at her from the foot of her bed, spying on her and judging her every move from my dreams.

She was a tough chick. He hadn't realized how tough when they were sneaking around behind my back, treading softly on my footprints so as not to be suspected. She had blown up our house, had blown it down, had burned it to the ground.

I withdrew, exiled myself to the island to find what I had lost of myself and the pieces of "me" I had yet to find.

That's when the search began for my mirror image, my similitude, to see who I might be. But as I looked behind into the glass wall of the future, I found I was inclined to see before me into the past. Like in *It's a Wonderful*

Life, I wanted to know how the hand of life played out with no me, to see the place that I had held, my trace, like the soft rumpled cushion of a reading chair when no one's sitting in it any longer. Even if she did attempt to abolish me, *something* had to remain, an essence, *my* essence, and that is what I wanted to find.

I searched out the closest cyber café and googled him. I cyber-stalked him. I MapQuested her. I had once met a narcissist specialist who assured me that those who wish not to be found know how to avoid it. They can hide deep within themselves. They pay officials to keep them under the radar. They pay to be left off the MapQuest grid—their streets hidden, dark. If someone doesn't want to be found, ways *do* exist to satisfy the need for privacy, even today with surveillance cameras everywhere. I expected there would be black matter in the place of narcissistic Rene. Wrong!

I MySpaced him, and he had posted photos of himself with his arms wound around me, thick ropes of arms tying us together forever—there in cyberspace—and Whistler rubbing against us, declaring animal ownership. Photos were posted of her, too, smiling and fearlessly staring straight into my eyes, and photos of other women, friends, lovers, cats, dogs, alliances, some that I'd heard him mention, others that were alien to me, peculiar people. *This is a life,* I thought. *At one point I imagined I was at the center of it; soon after, I thought I was nothing; but here I see I am in it, we're all in it, in life.* Then I saw two dates with a small dash connecting them, two swinging gates, opening and closing. *Rene is gone,* I thought, *Rene is dead—he is the one missing from life.*

I touched my body to assure myself that I inhabited my space. My hands resting on my belly. Creativity. *Birth. Letting go. Going.*

***

Or maybe I'm not doing the story justice. Maybe I do find Rene. We meet at the cyber café over coffee and stories about old times. He tells me life hasn't been the same since I left. He begs me to leave the island, to abandon my quest to reunite with Rona. He tells me that if I return to *my* life, *our* life, he'll keep me safe. He promises we'll be eternally happy as he gently draws my head to his chest and I hear the soft, steady pounding of his heart like the perambulations of the dreamers at the souvenir shop. Walking. Walking. Stepmother sweeping. Sweeping. And then the footfalls soften. And the sirens outside the café are deafening. I feel frozen air against my cheek. Downy hairs at the back of my neck stand at attention. No heart. No soul. Beat. There is no reading the book backwards. His obituary says he died in his sleep. His dog was licking his face when the ambulance arrived. His dog's name is Whistler. His girlfriend is caring for this giant chow chow as best she can, but no matter how she tries to tempt him to the dog run, he refuses, tenses his oversized puppy body and plays dead. All he wants is to dream, his paws simulating running, running, running somewhere, to someone, never arriving.

Chapter 12

There were no children.

I never wanted them.

Whereas most little girls play "mommy," I'd play "marine biologist." Probing brackish waters stirred my deepest maternal instinct. Whereas other little girls would convene around Barbie fashion mall playsets, Barbie horse stables, and her pink glamour garage, I found myself intoxicated by the surface tension between ocean and atmosphere, where rarely a solid object can be spotted and the only existing boundaries are walls of water.

My starter fish were guppies. Once my females would become uncharacteristically still, I'd begin preparing the birthing tank, which I'd fill with a fanfare of cheap, colorful plants for the fry to hide in so they'd be able to escape their mom's devastating, unsociable hunger. Remember, I experienced First Mother's biological anger, as primal as the primeval swamps from which we all arrived, and understand the hazards mothers can pose.

After guppies, I began breeding Siamese fighting fish. I learned about how to incubate them from a 63-year-old agoraphobic quiltmaker who had created a rogue fish army to enfeeble her abusive husband. You'd be surprised by how easy these fighters are to propagate.

My most difficult and satisfying offspring, by far, have been koi. The pond must be decorated with delicate plants such as water hyacinths or oriental water grasses, gossamer-type sealife that dances in clear water, pliant plants that attract iridescent dragonflies. Koi are works of living art. Observing and then mimicking their serene lifestyle has bettered mine, and I like to believe that I have helped them, too, that ours has been a mutually ameliorating friendship.

So, no, I never wanted screaming babies. And Rene and I didn't have any.

When Father and Rona ran off together and I was overwhelmed with a spontaneous belief that something was rapidly growing inside of me, the idea that I was pregnant couldn't have been more—I want to say "unexpected," "unsuited to me," only words with the prefix "un" come to mind—undesirable.

The sky was growing darker and the moon peered over the pier, preparing to dip into the cool drink below. The day had been long and now, with the nearing nether-belly of time, I needed to find a bed, a clean place to dream.

The boardinghouses by the loading yard off the wharves abound with fishermen, drunks, stevedores, and seafarers, the kind of men I grew up around. Amenities are not discussed in such hovels. I saw a handpainted sign in which the image of a raven was deftly carved, and I prepaid for a room there.

As I lay in bed, drifting in the waves of pre-sleep, the sea scents permeating the air, water clapping against water outside the window, pictures and sounds of my father, my stepmother, Rene, and Whistler flashed and crashed before me, and if a shaman had appeared at that moment, informing me that I was entering the realm where those who have passed over preside, I wouldn't have flinched. But what did astonish me was that by my side was a teeny version of me—could I have given birth? Was there a breeder involved, in the same way that I had carefully created perfect conditions for my precious koi?

There were earth-divers plunging into the collective unconscious. There were mediators, translators who fluently, fluidly spoke languages of the varying realms. There was chaos, not the kind that makes the day seem out of sorts, but dramatic cosmic eruptions. And there were superhero birds, diving through air, diving through me, as though I were air.

"Is it a bird? No, it's Superman."

Are you a bird? Are you my mother?

Superman, the shiny man of steel with his dull sidekick self, the journalist. Superman, the one who makes news and the other who writes about it. Are they opportunists, or what? Could Superman exist without Clark Kent—the witness, the scapegoat, the slapstick bumbler, the Cyrano de Bergerac for Lois Lane—the writer?

Earth-plungers and superheroes. I fell off the flattened earth, arrived at its end.

Chapter 13

In a vase by my bedside was a bouquet of dream flowers, the same kinds that Rene would buy for me: *Linnaea boreali* (commonly known as twinflower), sundog yarrow, and toxic delphiniums with their thousand flowers fanning like hands of cards, the flower whose petal juice, when combined with alum, presents as blue ink.

"Write me a secret letter and drop it in a dead letter box," was Rene's last request, as I was walking out his door. Now that he's dead, his plea sounds pining, a petition for me to find him after he is no longer findable. Then I think of Rona's appeal, "I want you to help me find your twin. Will you do what I ask of you? I need you to be in two locations at once."

And there I was, somewhere largely outside logic, in the heart of a moment omen with meteor-sized doubts dive-bombing meat eaters, back with Mu Qing, my stevedore father, Rene, Whistler, and Rona, the crew, staring into First Mother's glass belly vase where I swam/flew into the eyes of dream flowers and I am the thousand leaves, the mille-feuille, elongated crystals, flat crystals, wobbling crystals, yes, crystals from the glass womb, the sweet sunshine my stepmother would sweep when she was a young woman in grayish work pants and a lab coat, the poems my father recited as he rowed toward god through fog, Rene's yellow yarrow flowers that follow me, his irises that stare me down, Whistler guarding my reed basket and Rona, my other half, the twin sister that I was promised, whom I have never trusted, my slanted self, my shadow half, the bloodsucker.

It is important to know that pandas are bears that often give birth to twins and that one of the twins is usually rejected by its mother. Rejection is part of the bearing process.

Women from the Yoruba tribe of Nigeria tend to give birth to twins (called *ejire*—"two who are one") who bring them luck, though twins who are temperamental are said to be fated for disaster. When a jinxed twin dies, the grieving mother is consoled with an *ere ibeji*, which is a delicately carved satinwood replacement baby that has a cowrie chest-plate. The mother nestles her pointy-headed *ere ibeji* on her back, close to her heart. She loves it as though it were alive, as though she herself were dead. As mysterious as the high twin birth rate is, the twins' towering mortality rate is even more inexplicable—twins stealing the breath of the competition, hawking breathless bodies as collectables, live and nonlive Yoruba infants ripping out siblings' souls to sell them on the black market. I know about this ritual because I visited a strangulated soul in a museum, saw the condensation, its tears fogging the glass showcase.

What if I'm the nonrejected twin panda and the other, Rona, has shapeshifted into a spy? She is the *ere ibeji* cast on Mother's back to witness the future as it unfolds. The Watcher/The Seer. I look in the mirror and see Rona/see Nora. I touch my arms. They are not me. I touch my breasts. No, not me. My Jacobson's organ. No. My light. My lungs. Always two, similar patterns recurring progressively to describe random phenomona such as fluid turbulence, galaxy formation. Fractals. Perfect expressions of love.

Paddling toward the light, toward the lighthouse, walking into the blinding light so as not to face our dependence and the yawning distance between who has what and who has nothing.

The ancient Sufi poet Attar wrote, "Soldier, throw your clothes to the ocean." Fighter, abandon your false armor. Friend, surrender!

From the window of the Black Raven rooming house, I look out over the wharf and see a double rainbow and the sea transforming into a fish and a fish streaming into an ocean, as I'm breaching into sleep, loosed, slipping into bed, a bed made of tones, and stones, and storms, sea where halibut is served on a metabed of weed—the process of death that lasts our entire lives.

"Waveless in its bed the ocean lies," wrote Petrarch.

Now that I've left the island and I'm on the mainland, living in the Black Raven, I realize that Rona and Rene are on the land as well as in the water, that to find them I must bilocate on the surface tension.

Chapter 14

The Black Raven was built in the 1700s during the menhaden fishing industry boom. The Seafarer's Church, Sadie's Tavern, and the Black Raven were erected the same year. Boom, boom, and boom.

There was an adage in the day that proclaimed that, upon going ashore, every sailor was destined to hit each of the three ports in a twenty-four-hour haul—ports of refuge. My first port of call had been the Black Raven, where I had expected a night of deep sleep. Instead, for no reason, at least none that I am privy to, Death had had me in its jaws. But right then, when Death was considering me for dessert, when the world was preparing to close up behind me, it spit me out! Not only was I spared death, but I gave birth, or better said, birth had been given to me in the shape of a miniature. When I awoke in a rush from my death (or birth), a vase of flowers—the variety that had been brought to me by Rene—appeared magically by my side, a blooming note of lavish delphinium blue had been placed on my commode. There, woven in dream fabric, was a trace from Rene and Rona for me to find, to help me find them—to help me split into two, the two that I am.

I googled the keyword "raven" and read: *Pagans find ravens to be intelligent by nature, fluent in all "human" languages, tool users. The raven carries one type of death that is one type of birth brought by the raven. They transport messages from other worlds/realms. The black raven is a hidden, mystical storage center of lost instinct and hermetic wisdom. Sailors would rather kill their mothers than a raven. Priests turn into ravens after death, turn to ravens, raving. Ravens gather on a full moon and fill the light with blackness. Ravens find that which is hidden from sight.* Lastly, I read, *She who rests near a cave of ravens will travel beyond her wildest dreams.*

As I read about ravens—picturing raven hair, raven eyes, ravens' call to arms, armless ravens dressed in tuxedos, careless ravens aiding sailors on seas in which surface tension allows water striders to skate and humans to amble on air like gliding ravens, ravens as guides through the underworld—I began to remember an idea I had come across when reading a Stephen Hawking book, that everything—from prehistoric bugs to fully developed civilizations—is sucked up by black holes and documented on the horizon's skin and then irradiated back as a hologram, a shadow. Therefore, pixelated, digitalized computer images are real, while actors are residual totems. The bright star in the dead night sky. A butterfly's dream. I'm flying on a black raven's back and what feels like "I" is a tattoo of a bird on biceps.

Sadie's or the House of the Sailing Lord? I wondered. My stomach cawed like a hungry raven, which answered that question. *Sadie's it is.* I imagined my miniature loosed from me, free to follow her own narrative. I put on my black cloak and with hair wrapped in a snood, I walked down the block to Sadie's Tavern. On my way, I saw a migrating monarch butterfly heading toward the shipyard.

There she was with her pitted blue hellhole door and a tarnished brass latch. I did have an idea of what land lay on the other side of the door. Imagination is a prickly beast. It tends to color what's seen. When what you have imagined and what you see are one and the same, it's natural to grow suspicious of what appears before you. I was suspicious. I was seeing exactly what I imagined Sadie's to be. And as though Sadie's had eyes, she was seeing me. She, the tavern, was "some unknown but still reasoning thing" (from *Moby-Dick*). She took my breath away.

A tavern can be a living entity with essence and functioning organs. A tavern can disappoint or far exceed expectations. You can rest your hopes on a tavern. Upon opening the creaky door of Sadie's Tavern, after spending a dream-filled night at the Black Raven, there was no question that I was exactly where I was meant to be. There, sitting at the corner table, were Rene and Rona, whispering to one another, a votive candle flickering under their chins, lighting their eyes, the scarce amount of light needed to allow for their dark thoughts to be seen. I looked and I knew. I looked and I didn't know. Peek-a-boo. Betrayal wears masks. Denial and Betrayal, life partners. A blind Oedipus. Tiresias. Milton and his daughters. Borges and his mother. Blind heroes and duplicitous prophets. In Sadie's, the flickering candlelight illuminated the way for me to see mine.

Sadie's Tavern is a forbidding place. Its patrons are blind. Once seated at the bar, you forfeit memories of the loved ones who have grounded you, have kept you anchored. You become the carefree soul that you had always wished you were but who threatens your equanimity.

Amnesiacs can conceive of no autobiographical future, can preserve no past. Memory's constructive nature coincides with the imagination. When the brain is in the elaboration phase or new moon, it is scrambled, there is no continuity—of self or others. There's not conscience, there are no corners.

And without corners there are no directional points. Sometimes someone is punished before she commits the crime, vomits before drinking grog. Memories can work both ways, like time. Punishment and crime. Memories can forget. They can stand up and walk out of your life. You can implore them to stay, like a lost lover, only to realize years after the fact that your paramour had left long before you took notice. *You*, too, had left long before you had noticed.

Standing at the threshold of Sadie's, I was balancing at the still point, the fulcrum, at which past, present, and future hold court and all bets are off.

The rounded walls of Sadie's Tavern grew darker, then lighter. No longer did I only see Rene and Rona plotting, now there was my father, the stevedore, sitting with them, between them. I saw him hand Rona the porcelain key from the trinket shop and point to where I thought I was.

The last months that Rene and I were together I call The Year of Decoupage. At that time, I began to assemble stray photographs from when we first met, stamps removed from postcards he had sent me throughout the years, swatches of material from favorite furniture and clothing. I'd glue these fragments onto boxes—all types of boxes, all sizes—and seal them with layers of varnish. I let no judgment about the type of box I used interfere with my decoupaging—tampon boxes, tissue boxes, icebox boxes (what doesn't come in a box?), boxes made from wood, tin, paper, and plastic. The Year of Decoupage started out as a hobby and quickly turned into an obsession. My habit of decoupaging became so consuming that Rene would beg me to stop, threaten me, and sometimes even hide my materials. But the beauty of decoupage is that a box is on every street corner; so no matter how effectively he thought he was cutting off my supply, I could always get more. By the time I left Rene, I had built a labyrinth of boxes, empty and leading nowhere, a labyrinth of invisible pathways. When I walked out the door, I took only one box with me, a tiny wooden container that was decoupaged with three photographs—one of Rene on the night we met, one of Stepmother dressed as a mermaid (a Halloween costume), and the third one of me, taken by me, looking into an antique looking glass, a backwards me that looks like Rona. Chips of a mirror that had winked at a full moon and had captured a remarkable volume of night's light surrounded the lacquered photos. The rest of my decoupages I relinquished. I have no doubt that my boxed set of history was destroyed by his next "me." I have, at times, wondered what prompted me addictively to save snippets from a relationship that couldn't be saved, but that I hadn't yet acknowledged I would soon be leaving. Nor has the irony been lost on me that by building a museum to my past, I had made it ridiculously easy for my replacement to destroy all my mementos.

I've placed Whistler's ashes in my small, remaining decoupaged box. When I'm having trouble falling asleep, I cover the box with a soft piece of dark fabric, black as a moonless night—the light radiating from the mirror chips can be that terribly bright.

The memory of The Year of Decoupage washed over me as I watched my father point to me in Sadie's as though I weren't there, as though I were a fading memory, a decoupaged container. Confusing! A burly, bearded man in the booth next to them was involved in an intense conversation with an agitated beauty, his peasant bread sandwich untouched in front of him. Since no one at Sadie's seemed to take notice of me, I grabbed the sandwich and walked over to Rene, Father, and Rona's booth, sitting down quietly beside them, chomping and listening.

Rona held the porcelain key with blue sailboats on it that Father had just given to her. She said, "The bruja gave Nora this key to help her. I'm sure of it. I bought one just like it. Each replication that's sold supposedly has exactly the same powers as every other one, only the cost to the buyer is different."

When Rona articulated an observation, I noticed that she stated it as though it were a fact. She was the professional spy in the crowd. She had written a book on it. And she had the confidence; a bit of a confidence man, she was. Father and Rene nodded their heads in unison like bobblehead dolls. I had to stifle a laugh. What I found odd, though, was that I wasn't sure who Rona was talking about. I was at the store when the cashier sold the key to the little girl, her father waiting for her at the door. But now I understood Rona to say that *I* was given the key at the store, the key to something I didn't yet know about.

"So, I figure if we find out what the key is for, we'll find her."

Yes, I concurred, very much looking forward to be found.

Rene seemed restless and I felt the jim-jams as I watched his nervous leg jittering. "Why'd she go off on her own?" Rene asked this question as though I had broken a cardinal rule by taking off in a cardinal direction.

"Don't worry; the girl can take care of herself. I've been watching her closely for years. I was standing at the entryway of the store when she was given that key, you know. I was very proud of her." Father looked at his sun-stained hands and continued, "After her stepmother died, she was compelled to go on a walkabout. She told me so."

"When?" Rene asked.

"She talks to me, without even knowing it. Sometimes when she's alone, she'll say something from her heart and what she says reaches me. Can't explain it better than that."

As I listened to Father talk about the way we communicate, I became mindful of how, since his death, I have felt him on a cellular level. The day Stepmother finally surrendered to her bone-tired body, I threw out all my shoes and took to bed. If it hadn't been for Father, I would never have gotten through the loss. He'd playfully pull my hair just as I was falling off to sleep. He'd send Whistler into my dreams to nibble my elbow. He even orchestrated a plumbing disaster—bursting pipes, flooding kitchen—that I did nothing about. Days later, my stepsister, serendipitously, showed up at my door with her emergency plumbing tool kit and a pair of loafers that she deposited by the welcome mat. "Dad gave me these for you," she said—after fixing my pipes—as she closed the door behind her. Then she stuck her head in to yell, "And don't forget the bread, milk, and ham," before she locked up after herself.

I recognized Rene's need to disengage as he looked around the tavern for some emotional escape—a story he could embellish out of a couple's furtive glances or a shy woman sitting alone at the bar reading a book, whom he might be able to flirt with. He hated not being the writer of the show. Rona and Father couldn't tell that he wanted to be anyplace but here, but I could; I could still read his thoughts. I placed my hand over his. I felt his body heat on my palm and saw his cheeks brighten slightly, though he didn't look at me. Not one of them looked at me. Was I there? I couldn't tell. They didn't seem to think so, of that I was sure.

I thought of the Rene whom I believed I had known, the Rene and Nora who I was convinced were as intimate as two people could be.

During first coffee in the mornings, we'd call a "family meeting," to keep each other abreast of our missions and desires. They were the daily glue of our venturing out into discrete worlds. Only I hadn't realized, or admitted, that his world had been shared intimately with another. Only I hadn't realized that an underlying reason for the family meeting was so that he wouldn't run into me when he was with her. After I had left him, I would sometimes play the part of him in my mind to help me understand how he could emotionally survive his illegal easement, carry his love over me, like electrical lines passing over property, to another, how he must have felt calling me in the middle of the day after *they* made love in our bed to tell me how much he loved me. Whistler must have known what was going on, a thought that saddened me.

The porcelain key rested on the table between the three of them. The girl who runs toward voices. *Is she somewhere in me? Am I her?* I wondered. How close and far are we all from one another? The lies of connection.

I listened to Father, Rona, and Rene mumble softly. I imagined that I was each of them. First one, then the other, the me that was them and the me that was me alone, so far from them that they couldn't see me, *the me too far away to see.* A warm feeling. A color-saturated feeling. A B-sharp feeling. I thought of Oedipus trying to get home and achieving his goal, meeting his maker, his mother, and loving her, learning the destiny of his father, and how finding home finally destroyed him, that throughout his life he was moving toward his destruction; he was always home. *Am I on a walkabout, as my father said I said? Or am I in Sadie's Tavern with three blind spies who are the deepest parts of me and the deepest mysteries to me? Who are they— these strangers whose books I've read a very small portion of? Maybe they are a part of the walkabout, tracks of dreams or dreaming tracks, songlines, singing dreams creating, sweeping. Part mortal/part immortal.*

I looked at my feet. I was wearing loafers.

Chapter 15

The Aboriginals of Australia walk the Footprints of the Ancestors, sing the land into existence. There the scorched desert radiates the Earth's heartbeat. Here/There. In Dreamtime, here is there. Dreamtime heroes, such as Lizard Dreaming, Turtle Dreaming, and Native Cat Dreaming, are bound in a territorial relationship of reciprocity. These Dreaming Spirits travel the land, creating rocks, trees, animals, everything that is seen and not seen—a musical composition, a symphony of totemic life. Shared dream. Sacred dream. Trails of words and notes along footprint lines. Lines of prints playing a deep Earth song. The song is a map. It prints the land. The land is the score. Its scores are scored. Songsters, the Dreaming Spirits, sing a parcel of land and pass the tune to the next Dreaming. The tune stays true and its taste is recollected in the melodic contour of land. Land's music is the memory bank for moving through space timelessly, mutable eternity. On a walkabout, the land is sung into existence. Each Dreaming Spirit song sung in a unique language, hundreds of Dreamings weaving through the Earth in totemic geography, hundreds of languages singing one song, handing over the shared song of creation, receiving, reciprocity.

Hollows of the Earth—its waterholes—are the Earth's eyes, looking up at the Dreamings who tread. Locked/Un- Earth's tears. The mouthless Earth that sees or sees not, blinded Earth. Wandering showers cleansing the eyes of Earth. Deep-land Ancestors sleeping in Earth's belly, boring through its waterhole eyes. Then back in. Withdrawing. Drawing within.

Here where the vast ocean swells, Spirit Dreamings dream of Water. Wet desert/dry desert/bottom of the ocean/top of the world. Today is a good day for seeing things—a double rainbow shapes the sky with a prism of light; turtle on the bottom of creation carries the Earth, is the Earth, and I saw her today, sang her today; and that hillock, too, ta-da; female monarch butterfly with a five-inch wingspan; and two fish leaping down/up varying heights—in figure-eight shapes. The Earth purrs and air vibrates and kneads my flesh, the music of a Jacobson's organ.

The labyrinth was not destroyed but pressed inside, burned into ideal glass, so clear, so true that its lines can't be seen, though sung, yes, its lines are sung, sung into present existence.

I jump into a waterhole, the 83% water that is my blood. Stepmother's arms wrap around my chest. I face the vast ocean and rest my weight against her small body, my hand hidden for extra protection in her armpit, my need to keep contact with her pulse, with her life, to keep my life. Stepmother is swimming me back to shore, singing me to safety. The buoyant water that embraces us, the mother that embraces me, the blood we share.

When Mu Qing vanished, I imagined she moved into the lighthouse. Now I swim on my own. I swim across the waves, across the current. I kick my legs the way Mu Qing taught me, my cheek resting on ideal glass, clear, invisible, reflective glassy water. The sun illuminates me, buoys me up. I am closer to Mu Qing than I've been since she has died. *Watch your P's and Q's,* she warns. *Bring bread, milk, and ham when traveling to unknown lands,* she advises.

I jump out of the waterhole and dry off. I've had enough; I shouldn't overdo, that's what Mu Qing would say.

Chapter 16

I looked up and Father, Rene, and Rona were gone.

Some moments lack continuity. Usually, I'm wearing the same clothes from one to the next. Usually, the person I'm talking to in one moment stands before me at the start of the subsequent one, even though I might be a perfectly new person and she might be new, too. Most often, moments don't appear to end, though of course they do. End and begin. Die and are born. This new moment at Sadie's, though, really *looked* new. When it was over, the triumvirate was gone. Maybe I should have been surprised that the laws of physics had been fractured. I wasn't.

I was in a booth in Sadie's Tavern, a generic country tune playing on the jukebox and some couples stomping in recognizable rhythms on the wood flooring. I didn't know the words to the song, but the melody sounded startlingly familiar. It brightened me. Buoyed me up. Through the window I saw a wren. My pals, though, were gone.

Next stop was the Seafarer's Church. As I started on my way, I noticed a shiny object under a table. The porcelain key. I placed it in the pocket of my jeans as though I were the girl who had followed voices, who had bought the key at the trinket store, as though my father watched from the portal, eminently proud, a traveler on the lookout for Scylla and Charybdis.

Insight/Confession: The *Times* article in which I read about Rona Z, the one that led to my search for her, the one that describes her groundbreaking research that had been presented in the paper given at the International Nonlinear Science Conference in Tokyo, was an obit. That's right. When I first picked up the newspaper that morning, I was so thrilled to read about Rona that I hadn't paid attention to why a newspaper article was being written about her in the first place. No, it wasn't intended to inform the public about electromagnetic fields that sometimes interfere with the functions of the temporal lobe, the collective representing a single group-mind, or to alert the *Times* readership of cutting-edge research on the changing attitudes of initiates of spycraft, but to apprise those who might care about the passing of a woman who affected the world in some small way, who affected me greatly.

A shape memory occurs when a surface becomes the same temperature as the submerged waters, the submerged, repressed unconscious.

Now, like a hurricane at sea, accumulating strength and speed from warm waters, the memory of reading Rona's obituary overwhelmed me, bands of thunderclouds spiraling through my thoughts that sped up and slowed down, building strength, confusing waters, disorganizing waves. Rona had died in a riptide, a lusty flow of water near shore had dragged her body off, never to be found and never to be buried in earth.

"It's the calm waters you need to be careful of," Stepmother would scream at me when I'd be playing peacefully with pails of sand by the water's edge. "You can drown in a teaspoon of water," she'd remind me on every trip to the shore.

One hundred deaths a year are caused by riptides, more than by most other natural disasters except for floods. In water we're born, in water we die! Eighty-three percent of it dilutes our blood. Riptides result in 18,000 rescues a year by lifeguards. There was no lifeguard on duty when Rona Z was pulled out by the arms of the ocean, drawn into wide open water, no one on guard to temporarily suspend her destiny. She moved through the fog, impenetrable fog, inexhaustable, immeasurable. The first book that she wrote detailed how to find what appears lost. People, articles of clothing, expensive jewelry. I practically memorized that book, a classic in spy literature. Rona had appeared lost to me and thanks to the *Times* article, I had found her. And through finding her, I had found Father and Rene. Then, deep memories rose from a primeval swamp of memory and, with them, the clarity that, in relative time, the three of them are dead—Father, Rene, and Rona too.

To balance life force, the mean sea surfaces increase, waves propagate over a gap that does not break and a powerful flow ensues, ripping loved ones away from home, away from mind. That's how it happens. Rona's death was ripped from my mind and then returned to shore. The Seafarer's Church. I needed to offer my respects to Rona.

As I was leaving Sadie's, I glanced into the mirror that hung above the door. A science experiment that has always fascinated me asks the subject to look at a blank screen while thinking about a green pattern. The subject is given red-green glasses and then is asked to look at a different screen with one green and one red pattern projected onto it. The green pattern is visible to one eye and the red image to the other eye. The longer that one has spent imagining the green pattern, the more likely she will see it. The experiment demonstrates that what we imagine influences what we see. I was reminded of this as I glanced at my face, my expression, my grim determination. What was I imagining and what was I seeing? What did I imagine I would see? A middle-aged woman searching for mother and child—past and future?

"Useless to ask a wandering man advice on the construction of a house. The work will never come to completion," Stepmother liked to remind me. Yes, Stepmother. Maybe Confucius was right.

Once upon a time, a princess was born who was as dark and translucent as her own shadow, and who had eyes that were beacons of starlight. Her father was the mighty Poseidon, the powerful sea god who watched over every single one of his trillions of children, which he had fashioned as the sea and stone. After the little princess's mother died (fairy tales are all about the ones you love dying and abandoning, making bad choices, adrift at sea), Poseidon gave her to the Queen of Panthera, or the Native Cat Dreaming, along with a giant ball of twine that unwound in the winds, measuring, defining space and time. The stepmother and daughter could live peaceably and simply as long as the twine remained secure, but it was the cat's nature to unwind the giant ball. And play she did. And the princess? She, too, unwound, unwound the giant ball of thick thread and filled the sky with shadow and light. Unbeknownst to her, she had a mirror sister, who was lightning. So she, her father the Sea, her stepmother the Cat spirit, and her sister, who was electrically charged, permeated space and time, perfumed space and time. One complete world.

I fixed my eyes on the pattern of my face, the light and shade. The proportion of who I am in a mirror.

Yoni is the Sanskrit word that refers to something that has been stored in the womb during the first two weeks of pregnancy, when past, present, and future, like a ball of string, a continuous stream, are gathering steam, are a vacuum sucking matter in and out of every direction and corner of life energy, movement. The moment in the mirror, in the forest, when trees and air and voice and the hollows, the hollering, inside and out, are flattened and stunningly whole, stunningly simple. Whistler leaping into the forest when his services were no longer needed.

The heart of the port town is the Seafarer's Church, built in Georgian Revival style, and with its bays, pedimented dormers, and monumental pilasters, the structure is symmetrical, rich with classical detail. The building promises to remain fixed on land for transient mariners. A fresco of Saint Elmo, his eyes poked out, adorns the walls of the chapel's wings. Some believe that after Erasmus of Formiae or Saint Elmo, as he is popularly called, escaped from the Roman Emperor Maximian, ravens fed him, kept him from dying (for a while anyway), until he was recaptured and his intestines were wound around a windlass; hence, he has become the patron saint of sailors.

I proceeded to the back of the church and watched the seafarers wander about restlessly like scrambling sandpipers outrunning whitewater, like sandflies, mollusks, singly, in pairs, in small groups of four or five, seeking solace or rest in perpetual motion. *Living without purpose,* I thought. A hum was emitted by their hairy, moist flesh, thick with sweat and the stench of beer and smokes, men on shore leave, a transient group in search of a storm. Nomadic tribes attaining permanent peripatetic conditions, rooting around for permanent summer, spring, or endless winter. *Ask none of these men how to build a home*, I thought. *These sailors are continually reorienting themselves in relation to some shifting interior sky filled with universes of North Stars.*

A cool blue light blew in from the corner of the outmost reaches of the chapel's clerestory windows. I followed it with my eyes and saw that it bent away from the streams of wandering seamen and led to a room that was partially hidden from view. Lucid from light. Tranquil. I walked toward it, toward the light, not in a wayless way, yet not knowing where I was heading; nevertheless, I headed there with surety. Buddha supposedly said something like "You cannot travel on the path before you have become the path itself." His last words to his disciples before dying have been recorded as "Walk on!" The man who was all about sitting extolled the rhythm of walking, walking away from what one believes. I stood at the entrance of the side chapel, looking into the lighthouse.

"So that was the Lighthouse, was it? No, the other was also the Lighthouse. For nothing was simply one thing. The other Lighthouse was true, too…In the evening one looked up and saw the eye opening and shutting and the light seemed to reach them in that airy sunny garden where they sat," so wrote Woolf.

Chapter 17

Sitting in the pew of the chapel was Stepmother and the miniature "me" by her side. Frankincense and myrrh filled the air. I thought of Ferlinghetti's "whitebone drones…among hallucinary moons," of his "two streams / which are the twin streams / of oblivion," as I looked disbelievingly at the two apparitions that I have known so well. I might even have shaken my head to try to wake up from the dream. How cliché.

I don't think I've mentioned my stepmother's passion for the color blue. Everything she had owned was blue. When she'd return from a day of shopping and I'd ask her what she bought, she'd thoughtfully describe the tones of the objects rather than tell me what they were. So, for instance, she might say "iris, turquoise, ultramarine, royal," rather than "scarf, garbage pail, some curtains, a pair of leather gloves for you."

There, in the side chapel, my stepmother was dressed in an electric blue cinched shift with periwinkle chiffon sleeves. The outfit she was wearing was *so* Mu Qing that I couldn't possibly have contrived it; she had to be sitting there in the flesh. And the little girl who sat next to her, my miniature, wore the same dress as she, just like when I was a kid and my stepmother dressed us like carbon copies in Mommy and Me mix-and-matches, two impossibly different shapes cut from the exact same cloth. I felt like singing.

"New babies have an appetite for forward motion, like sharks," Mu Qing said without looking at me, the miniature me, propped up against her heart.

I hugged our stepmother, the only true mother I had known.

She looked at me. Her eyes foggy, she continued, "Your screams: your streams of screaming, your fear of the dark..." My miniature took up Mu Qing's train of thought, "...fear of strangers, terror of things..."

I began to sing. The music of birds, the liquid song of tree swallows. The wren. Mockingbird. The melody of birdsong flying through me. Sometimes I can sing and talk and scream all at once, and other times I close my mouth like a locked jail door. Both can be pleas for help.

"Stepmother, help."

"Once upon a time, when fairy tales were headlines: 'Wolf Eats Granny and All the Silly Dwarfs in the Forest.' 'Nuclear Proliferation.' 'Genocide.' There was a time that the archenemy stalked us from inside. Slept in us. A time when the archenemy dressed up as our desires—a candy house, a hot young man, a restful night's sleep. A time, too, when stepmothers poisoned their words, I mean wards."

"Stepmother."

"There was a time when our compulsions drove us out of our right minds, into our night minds. Who understands instinct?"

"Help."

"Our instinct to run, to protect, our instinct to live, and what we are willing to kill in order to live."

"Help."

The little girl beside Mu Qing chanted, "Whoever wishes to quickly afford protection to both herself and others should practice the holy secret: the exchange of self for others. May I be a boat, a bridge, a passage for those desiring the farther shore."

"Help," I called as loudly as I could, though the sound from my throat hardly escaped, like the ringing of a bell buoy dissipating in the empty ocean air. No one could hear my meek cry, I was sure.

"Help," squeaked through my throat, as though I were pushing a newborn sound out of the vaginal canal of a dream.

I was in the ocean, alone and in danger of being alone. I was in the desert on a walkabout. Thirsty and vanishing. Vanquished. I was sure I was alone.

"Help, Stepmother." I stretched out my arms toward the small me, breathed her into my lungs, into my heart. She extended inside and outside. She was the water, the air, rising and falling.

I felt hands reach for me. Small hands of children. Rough hands of sailors. Stepmother was helping me, Whistler, too. And I was helping those that surrounded me, buoying them up. Aloft. Alight. *Help,* we all sang out as one.

Chapter 18

A crescent blood-orange-hued moon lit my way once I left the chapel. The night air stank of salty oak-barrel beer, invisible worlds undetectable to the human eye, though present nevertheless. I thought I saw the soft glow from the constellation Corvus and heard a raven in the far distance. An overwhelming sense of gratitude. *How well do I know the air? How well do I know my own mind?* I wondered.

Before returning home, on my way to port, I decided I would stop at the souvenir shop to see the silvery witch, to say thanks. Once outside her shop, I noticed that the structure's substantial windows allowed the warm yellow and green glow of the place to blanket the walkway around it. The form of the building appeared like the aurora borealis itself; the patrons inside as shadows in a cave of light. Passing by me, as I gaped at the store, was a procession of Tibetan monks, wrapped in saffron and maroon robes, with yellow-fringed high hats like horses' manes. The first in line held a vessel that was swaddled in a patchwork cloth sewn from pure-tone silk. I watched the monks stream toward the water, carrying with them a sand mandala—a complex cosmic blueprint of palace gates, palace walls; the highest planes of consciousness; a sweet song of the Buddha; the conflagration of delusion, of self; a million grains of sand—and toss it into the current of energy for the benefit of all beings, sand flowing into water, extinguishing fire, transforming sand to shell, to stone.

The thunderbolt is the protective ring. Hear it gong! Ripples passing through time. A wind gathered from some other place and night clouds covered up the moon. The rain poured out of the sky. I ran inside the store for protection.

Bone-littered earth symbolizes our impermanence. Our flesh flexing. The weather report conveys impermanence.

Our animals exemplify our passing. Sails catching air.

Inside the store nothing was out of the ordinary, out of place. The tourists scoured the shelves, looking for their unique selves projected onto mass-produced junk, while the key and cowries were stuffed in the deep seas of my pockets. I was about to place them carelessly on the wrong shelves and catch the first ferry back to where I'm from when the proprietor, the santera, snuck up behind me and asked if she might be of help.

"Here," I said, placing the contents of my pockets into her hands, like a child caught in the act of finding things before they're lost.

"Flashlights." She looked down at the porcelain key and the shells that she now held.

I had no idea what she was talking about. *What flashlights?* I thought to myself.

"There. Here." She smiled at my innocence, which made me defensive. Then she said, by way of an explanation, "The key and cowries flashed a light on you, showed your family where you were. So they could help you. So you could help them."

"Yes."

"Good of you to return these items. Some people hold on to things for way too long." The santera handed me a pack of cards. "You used to enjoy playing as a child."

"Of course." I smiled. "Only I was wrong," I said as I walked out the door.

"Yes," I heard from behind me. On the street I handed the cards to a young man who reminded me of the guy from Brugge, a handsome twenty-something who still had years of self-constructed stories to live, meanings that he would create to justify his choices.

The store's light protected me all the way to the ferry and I whistled aloud, placing my right foot on one slick gray cobblestone that was part of the cobblestone road and my left foot on a silver stone, and my right foot on the ash cobblestone, and my left foot on the Russian blue stone, and my right foot on the smoky gray cobble, one foot, then one foot, walking on, whistling and singing each step into being.

Chapter 19

I didn't see my father when I boarded the ferry. My twin wasn't by my side. Much had changed in the past twenty-four hours. For one thing, I didn't feel alone, and I wasn't alone. The boat was filled with other travelers, fighting their way back home like me, moving toward—not a home from the past, but a fresh one—a momentary home.

The foghorn blew and before I knew it, we were riding the open seas. A woman my age, dressed all in blue (navy, cobalt, cerulean, Stepmother would say), toted a blue cat in a decoupaged carrier. *Could I make this up if I tried?* An older woman, who looked nothing like me, I might add, dangled from her thin wrist a charm bracelet that hosted a sky's worth of shiny silver birds, and if it wasn't exactly the jewelry that Rene meant for me, it was memorably similar. A schoolboy had in his hand one of the two books of poems that my father wrote, published many years ago. My father's author photo face up, a black and white of a stunning man working at the docks, looking exactly how I remember him from when I was eight or nine, how he'll eternally remain in my memory.

The ferry trip back was excruciatingly long. By the time the boat docked, I felt too exhausted to take one more step, though pressing on was a requisite, so press on I did.

The parking lot emptied out quickly. Such quiet. Waves against wood. A gentle rhythmic slapping. I would walk through the forested area to arrive back where I began, if such a place still existed. Lemon infused a light breeze. The moon pushed through the curtain of cloud, reasserting itself, one lone slit of a wolf's eye demanding to see.

I walked. The snood still held my bun, the cloak covered my jeans to midcalf, my loafers faced forward. Walking through the forest to complete my travels, I became everyone, everyone on the boat, everyone on all boats, and my guides were Rona, Father, Stepmother, Rene, Whistler, Sadie, the ravens and the fish, the wrens and the cats, the Watchers and the silvery witches…all me and all with me. I/We walked. I/We started singing softly, then louder and louder as the forest grew denser and denser:

To arrive anywhere intact

The composer must penetrate the forest. With his imaginaries,

His aura, aurally

The composer translates human praxis

Into vernacular knowledge,

Must pierce body and forest / fatty Earth and the thick bones of trees

*

The composer's imaginaries secrete space & spatial
          Underpinnings that support smaller and smaller forests,
          Microscopic forests, invisible forests

          (How do you tell the tale of a forest in absent land?)

Teeny ones full of ghosts and cold
Female composers low to the ground
Playing in color / with phantoms / bright dyes
& bright eyes—waterfalls offering water
To thirsty spirits

          Protean forests

          Supersized ones, spectacular spectacles
          Of colossal filigreed forests

*

Beware of criminal ghosts under house arrest in giant trees or housed
In the bodies of animals. A tree kangaroo might know too well
The forest's acoustics, an ancient specter dressed in marsupial skin
Hearing calls, the composer will write in the future

          To expand the experience of time
          To display an interior core

*

Even if song were a vehicle driven by frog and monkey,

Liberated from the dark/moist forest by the composer writing it into being,

Even if he were born with a dictionary

                                And primer specific to his clan's symbols,

Even if he were born with an instruction manual,

                                    Instructor's guide [answers], CliffsNotes,

Even then, the exegesis of the composer and his composition

                                                Would pass beyond

                                Sense

                        Ineffable,

                    Evanescent,

                        Even part mineral. Even part criminal.

    The spirit is indeterminate—random neurons—

                    Loose wires and red ribbons, unbridled

        [upbraided].

The flexible spirit escapes house arrest,

                    Travels wormholes through light years,

                        Pierces fatty Earth and thickened bones of trees,

Surfaces as the spirit of the forest,

                    The flesh of the forest,

                    The composer of the forest.

Acknowledgments:

Thanks to those who read an early draft of *2X²*: Kristine Faxon,
Kara Hartig, Rick Moody, David Rosenboom, and Matthew Sharpe.
Thanks to Andrea Biggs. Thanks to so many others. Thanks to
Geoffrey Gatza.

And I gratefully acknowledge the editors of *New American Writing*
and *VERSE* for publishing excerpts of this work.

And special thanks to Lindsey Brown, who led me to find this tale.

Made in the USA
Charleston, SC
27 March 2011